D0638813

The Clever Friend

by Kim Kane

Illustrated by Jon Davis

PICTURE WINDOW BOOKS
a capstone imprint

For my son George, who is first and foremost kind.
(Edgar, you've already had yours!)

— Kim

Ginger Green, Playdate Queen is published by Picture Window Books,
A Capstone Imprint
1710 Roe Crest Drive
North Mankato, Minnesota 56003
www.mycapstone.com

Ginger Green, Playdate Queen — *The Clever Friend*
Text Copyright © 2016 Kim Kane
Illustration Copyright © 2016 Jon Davis
Series Design Copyright © 2016 Hardie Grant Egmont
First published in Australia by Hardie Grant Egmont 2016

All rights reserved. No part of this publication may be reproduced in
whole or in part, or stored in a retrieval system, or transmitted in any
form or by any means, electronic, mechanical, photocopying, recording,
or otherwise, without written permission of the publisher.

Library of Congress Cataloging-in-Publication data
is available on the Library of Congress website.
978-1-5158-1951-6 (library binding)
978-1-5158-2019-2 (ebook PDF)

Summary: Ginger is playing with Meagan today. But what happens
when Meagan is a know-it-all? Can Ginger find a way for them
to play together?

Designers: Mack Lopez and Russell Griesmer
Production specialist: Tori Abraham

Printed and bound in China.
010734S18

Table of Contents

Chapter One

My name is Ginger Green.
I am seven years old.
I am the Playdate Queen!

Yesterday Meagan called.
She is my friend from school.

Meagan is in a different reading group, but she says we can still be friends.

Meagan said, "Hello, Ginger Green. Because it is summer vacation, I am allowed to have a playdate. Would you like to come over and play with me?"

Because I am Ginger Green,
Playdate Queen, I said,

"YES!"

Dad walks me to Meagan's house.
It is small and neat.

I knew Meagan's house would be
as neat as her desk at school.

Meagan's mom opens the door.
She looks just like Meagan. She
has the same glasses and the same
smooth hair. Meagan waves hello.

I fix my messy hair.

Dad fixes his messy hair too.
He gives me a kiss.

"Bye. See you in two hours."

I take off my shoes and walk
inside. There are books
EVERYWHERE.

There are more
books in Meagan's
house than in the
library. It is just as quiet.

I look around. I cannot
see a TV. "You have lots
of books and no TV," I say.

"I don't watch TV," says
Meagan. "It's not allowed.
I am only allowed to play
educational games."

"Oh," I say.

I am Ginger Green, Playdate
Queen, and I **LOVE** playdates.

I LOVE TV, and I LOVE games.

I wonder if my games
are educational.

Meagan and I go up to her
bedroom. I wait for Meagan
to suggest a game. She doesn't.
I wait longer. She still doesn't.
But that is OK.

I am Ginger Green, Playdate Queen, and I have LOTS of ideas.

I see a violin on the bed.

"You have a violin!" I say. "Let's play orchestra. I will be the conductor!"

I pick up
the stick.

"Don't touch
the bow!"

says Meagan.

"It is very delicate.
Touching the
bow can ruin it."

"Oh," I say again.

Meagan's house
makes me feel
like I should not
touch anything.

Meagan takes the bow and
picks up the violin.

"I need to practice my piece
for my recital," she says.
"It is very complicated."

Meagan plays a piece of music.
It sounds great.

Meagan puts the violin and
bow back in the case.

"Do you
play an
instrument?"
she asks.

"I play the shakers," I say.
"I made my own shakers
with rice and a cardboard
tube. I even
painted them."

"Shakers are not a
real instrument,"
says Meagan.
"A *real*
instrument
has music
and recitals."

I look down.
I feel bad.

"You should learn a real instrument," says Meagan. "Music is good for the brain. It gets the left side of the brain and the right side of the brain working together."

I do not tell Meagan that I get left and right mixed up. I do not tell Meagan that sometimes I still put my boots on the wrong feet. I do not tell Meagan that my left-side brain and my right-side brain are probably mixed up too.

Chapter
Two

I look at the pile of books near Meagan's bed.

"You have a lot of books," I say.

"I read **every** morning and **every** night," says Meagan. "I read all my books **twice**. What books do you read, Ginger Green?"

"My big sister, Violet, likes books,"

I say.

I like books too, but I do not read chapter books. I only read books with pictures. I am embarrassed to tell Meagan I cannot read such big books yet. I cannot read all the words.

Then I have another idea.

"I know! Let's play JUNGLE ESCAPE!"

I pick up some books and place them on the floor.

"The carpet is a raging river filled with hungry crocodiles. The books are stepping stones to freedom."

I JUMP onto the first book.

Then I JUMP to the next.

"We don't jump
on books in
this house,"

says Meagan.

"Oh," I say.

I get off the book. I see a hole in
the toe of my sock. I didn't notice
it before.

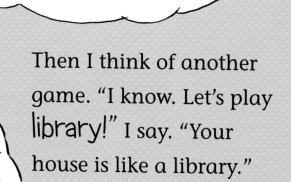

Then I think of another game. "I know. Let's play library!" I say. "Your house is like a library."

I put on Meagan's glasses. "I will be the librarian, and you can be the kid who wants to borrow books! Let's write numbers on the spines!"

I take a book from a pile. The book comes down, but so do ALL the books on top of it.

The door opens. Meagan's mom
looks at the books. She frowns.
"Girls, keep it down, please.
I am trying to work."

Meagan nods and
takes back her glasses.
"Sorry, Mom."

I start to pick up the books.

Meagan picks them up too.
"In my house we DO NOT
jump on books. In my house,
we DO NOT play pretend
with books. We *read* books,"
whispers Meagan.

"I have another idea."

I whisper.

"It isn't jumping on books, and it isn't playing pretend," I say. "Let's line up the books like dominos."

Meagan takes the book I am holding. She looks very angry.

"In my house, we don't jump on books," she says. "We don't play pretend. And we don't set books up like dominos. That is a **DUMB IDEA TOO**. Maybe if you just read books, you would be in my reading group."

Now I am angry too.

"Well, in MY house, we don't tell people their ideas are dumb," I say. "You might be clever, Meagan. You might be good at reading.

But you are NOT good at playdates. On playdates you don't make your friend feel bad. It is not clever, and it is not kind. If you make your friends feel bad, you will not have any friends at all."

I am not in Meagan's reading group.

And I do not want to be at
Meagan's house either.

"I AM GOING HOME."

Chapter
Three

Meagan looks at me.

"You are right, Ginger Green. I do not know what to do on a playdate. I do not know because I do not have many playdates. I am only allowed to have playdates during summer vacation."

Meagan looks like she is going
to cry.

"Please don't go, Ginger Green.
You are kind. And you actually
have great ideas. That is why
you are the Playdate Queen."

Meagan says this in a small
voice. Her big eyes look sad.

Meagan picks up a book.
"We could try book dominos,"
she says. "I have never done
that. If we use the paperback
books, they won't be so noisy."

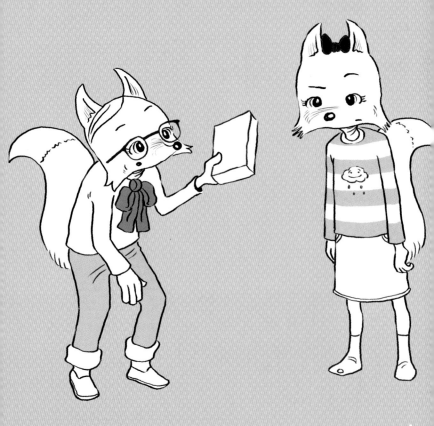

I sigh. Meagan was not kind. But she is being kind now. I have an idea. "If we're quiet we could line them up in the hall too. We could even go down the stairs!"

"That is a GREAT idea," says Meagan.

Meagan and I line up the books.

We line up the books in all
the rooms upstairs and
all the way DOWN
the stairs.

When we finally tip the books over, they fall neatly, one after the other.

They even do
LOOP-THE-LOOPS!

Meagan and I set the books
up again.

Then we watch them

TIP

through the house again.

We play CARDS!

We play

BAND.

Meagan plays the violin,
and I play the drums.

At four o'clock, the doorbell rings.

"Did they have a good time?" asks Dad.

"Well, they certainly had a noisy time!" says Meagan's mom.

"You should meet my sister Penny,"
I say. "She is **very** loud."

"I would love to,"
says Meagan.

"Would you like to come for a playdate at my house?" I ask.

"YES!"

screams Meagan.

"Meagan?" says Meagan's mom.

"Yes, PLEASE!" screams Meagan.

I laugh.

Meagan laughs.

The parents laugh too.

I am Ginger Green, Playdate Queen, and my friend Meagan is coming over next week. We are not in the same reading group, but we are still great friends.

We might play book dominos!
We might play cards.
We might even
make rice shakers
for our band.

Meagan
is very clever
at some things.

It turns out,
I am very
clever at some
things too.

THE END

Glossary

bow—a wooden rod with horsehairs stretched from end to end used in playing an instrument of the violin family

clever—smart or able to learn quicly

conductor—the leader of a musical group

orchestra—a group of musicians who perform instrumental music using mostly stringed instruments

pretend—to make believe

recital—a program of music usually given by a single performer

violin—a stringed musical instrument with four strings that is usually held against the shoulder under the chin and played with a bow

About the Author and Illustrator

Kim Kane is an award-winning author who writes for children and teens in Australia and overseas. Kim's books include the CBCA short-listed picture book *Family Forest* and her middle-grade novel *Pip: the Story of Olive*. Kim lives with her family in Melbourne, Australia, and writes whenever and wherever she can.

Kim Kane

Pirates, old elephants, witches in bloomers, bears on bikes, ugly cats, sweet kids — Jon Davis does it all! Based in Twickenham, United Kingdom, Jon Davis has illustrated more than forty kids' books for publishers across the globe.

Jon Davis

Collect them all!